Brilliant and Brown

Written by Candis Perdue

Illustrated by Phoebe Cho

13TH &
JOAN

For permission requests, write to the publisher, addressed "Attention: Permissions Coordinator," 205 N. Michigan Avenue, Suite #810, Chicago, IL 60601. 13th & Joan books may be purchased for educational, business or sales promotional use. For information, please email the Sales Department at sales@13thandjoan.com.

Printed in the U.S.A.
First Printing,

Library of Congress Cataloging-in-Publication
Data has been applied for.

ISBN: 978-1-953156-69-3

To every little Brown boy all
over the world who served
as my inspiration for writing
this book of affirmations.

Preface

Behind every adult is a powerful story that brought them to their current destination, though many never get the chance to tell that story.

There may have been a time when they needed just one person to believe in them, but instead that person shattered a spirit that had not yet fully bloomed.

The events that occur in this book, though written from the perspective of one little boy, happen to be the life and reality for many minority children.

I write this for anyone, young and old, whose childlike spirit was never watered or catered to. This book is for you.

Brilliant
and Brown

I was told by my mom I was Brilliant and Brown.

2

But once I got to school, it
turned out that what she
called brilliant, my teacher
said came "once in a million."

The words
Brilliant and
Brown, my mom spoke to
me each and every day.

But when I raised my hand to speak in class, the teacher would look the other way.

I tried to play with the
other kids but was picked
last for every game.

So I asked my mom, "if I'm so brilliant, why doesn't anyone call my name?

And why does it make me feel such shame?"

"Brilliant and Brown," was my mother's reply.

REPORT CARD

A+

10

"A true treasure and gift sent from the sky."

So what my teacher
thought came "once
in a million",

Is true character
and intellect.

Why do the other kids
choose to pick me last?

It is because I resemble
every bit of strength
from my ancestor's past.

"Brilliant and Brown," I repeat as I walk amid the crowd.

This description, I'll wear loud and proud!

13

Author Bio

In a world filled with tumultuous times of uncertainty, the one thing that author Candis Perdue feels will offer an escape and put one's mind at ease is a good book. Born and raised in Tampa, Fl., Candis Perdue is an English Language Arts educator, creative writer, life coach, and spoken word poet. She began writing short fictional stories during primary school. It was there where she learned that writing was not only a hobby, but also, according to one of her primary school teachers, a true gift and talent that she possessed. Candis would continue to write fictional stories throughout grade school, but it was during her high school years where she began to use her craft of creative writing to entertain friends and communicate the unspoken. Writing fictional stories soon developed into poetry and spoken word, and in turn, unconsciously became a therapy method that she later used to overcome low self-esteem and anxiety. Although her writing style reveals intimate feelings of self-doubt and self-worth,the shared insight embedded deep within her words not only allows the reader to empathize but also leaves them with encouragement, motivation, affirmation, and insight.

CPSIA information can be obtained
at www.ICGtesting.com
Printed in the USA
BVHW061443010622
638487BV00035B/90

9 781953 156693